My profound and delighted thanks to Khaled; Diop, his family, and Claire; Brahim; Alia; Khadija; Mina; Moctourna; Amina; Barry; Mahmoud, his sisters, and their mother; Isselmou; Erna and her family; Nagi; my English students; and friends, all of whom told me many wonderful stories and patiently explained their religion of Islam to me. —K.C.

To Behzad's childhood —H.H.

Text copyright © 2013 by Kelly Cunnane
Jacket art and interior illustrations copyright © 2013 by Hoda Hadadi

Visit us on the Web! randomhouse.com/kids

Educators and librarians, for a variety of teaching tools, visit us at RHTeachersLibrarians.com

Library of Congress Cataloging-in-Publication Data
Cunnane, Kelly.
Deep in the Sahara / Kelly Cunnane ; illustrated by Hoda Hadadi. — 1st ed.
p. cm.
Summary: An Arab girl of the Sahara who wants to wear a malafa,
the veiled dress worn by her mother and older sister, learns that the
garment represents beauty, mystery, tradition, belonging, and faith.
ISBN 978-0-375-87034-7 (trade) — ISBN 978-0-375-97034-4 (lib. bdg.)
[1. Coming of age—Fiction. 2. Clothing and dress—Fiction. 3. Muslims—Fiction. 4. Sahara—Fiction.
5. Africa, West—Fiction.] I. Hadadi, Hoda, ill. II. Title.
PZ7.C91625De 2013
[E]—dc23
2011050245

The text of this book is set in Filosofia.
Book design by Rachael Cole
The illustrations were rendered in collage.

MANUFACTURED IN CHINA
10 9 8 7 6 5 4
First Edition

DEEP in the SAHARA

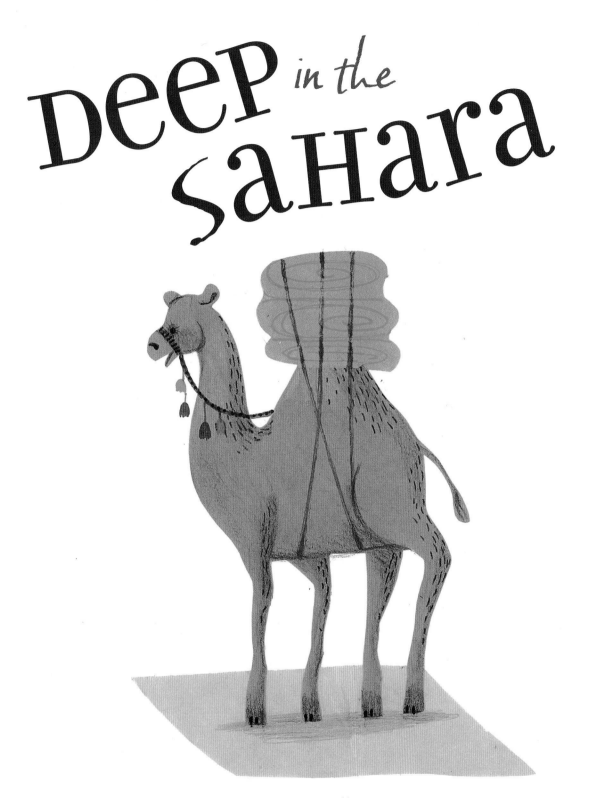

written by Kelly Cunnane · illustrated by Hoda Hadadi

schwartz & wade books · new york

Deep in the Sahara, sky yellow with heat, rippled dunes slide and scorpions scuttle.

In a pale pink house the shape of a tall cake,
you watch Mama's *malafa*
flutter as she prays.
More than all the stars in a desert sky,
you want a malafa so you can be beautiful too.

When you tell Mama, she smiles.
"Lalla, a malafa is for more than beauty," she says,
and her silver heels *tick tick tick* across the tiles.

Boys in turbans on donkeys go.

Men in white *boubou* stroll.

Your sister, Selma, in a malafa glows.

Nothing but dark eyes show.

More than all the camels in the land,

you want a malafa so you can be mysterious too.

When you tell Selma, she laughs.
"A malafa is for more than mystery," she says
as her flip-flops flip across the sand.

Women whisper on the corner, veiled head to toe
in malafa, color of lime and mango.
More than all the gold on a bride's crown,
you want a malafa so you can be a lady too.

When you tell Cousin Aisha, she pats you on the head
as if you're still a child!
"Lalla, a malafa is for more than being like us," she says,
and saunters away with the women through the dust.

Trees of red flowers bloom with heat.

Acacia pods rattle, and fruit bats sleep.

Grandmother sits on a cushion to brew tea,

her malafa the robe of ancient royalty.

More than all the mint leaves sold in the market,

you want a malafa so you can be like a long-ago queen too.

When you tell Grandmother, she hums, *Mmm.*
"A malafa is for more than old tradition," she says,
and gives you a glass to sip, minty and sweet with foam.

Goats waggle home to tents for milking, and
everywhere in the air is the evening call to prayer.
Men hurry to mosques,
and all the women to quiet places to pray—
except you.

"Mama," you say,

"more than all the dates in an oasis,

I want a malafa so I can pray like you do."

Mama stops and looks at you.

Then she gives one nod.

"*Zaiyn*. Good," she says, and gathers a malafa,

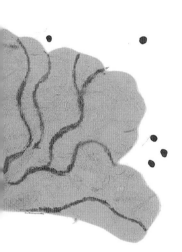

slips it over your head,

under your arm,

round and round—

a malafa,

as blue as the Sahara sky,

as blue as the ink in the Koran,

as blue as a stranger's eye.

"*Wahai.* Come," Mama says,
and climbs the stairs as the round white sun is falling
and the mosques are all calling.

And so you take a little step,
and then another,
up, up—
shwai shwai, little by little,
your malafa rippling down your back
and your arms and ankles like water.

Bats fill the sky.

The sun slowly dips behind the dunes,

and now, standing on the roof, you understand:

a malafa is for beauty,

a malafa is for mystery,

a malafa is for tradition

and belonging.

But even more, it is for something else.

"I know what a malafa is for," you tell Mama.

"A malafa is for faith."
And together, you face east,
your malafa fluttering behind like wings.

AUTHOR'S NOTE

Deep in the Sahara is set in Mauritania, West Africa, a country I lived in from 2008 to 2009. When I left the United States, I knew little about the faith of the Mauritanian people—only that they are Muslims, who practice the religion of Islam, that they pray five times a day and their holy book is called the Koran, and that Muslim women must wear a veil in public.

Each Islamic country differs in how strictly they practice their religious customs. In Mauritania, generally girls between the ages of nine and fifteen begin to wear a *malafa* for the modesty required by their faith and for protection from the sand and brilliant sun. Mauritanian men are covered with turbans, poncho-like *boubou,* and, often, enormous pants.

When the call to prayer is announced, Muslim people everywhere face their holy city of Mecca (in Saudi Arabia) to pray. Men and women pray separately at mosques; men may also pray in public groups, while women may pray in private or at home. This separation of men and women, and the custom of women wearing veils, is intended to keep a Muslim's focus not on the outer appearance of the body but on the inner, spiritual connection to God.

I went to Mauritania believing that the wearing of the veil was repressive to women, but the Mauritanians' relaxed and colorful expression of their faith and culture offered a surprisingly positive view, which I wanted to share by writing this book.

GLOSSARY

The people of Mauritania generally speak one of four main African tribal languages, and most people also speak French and a dialect of Arabic called Hassaniya. The words here are in Hassaniya.

Hassaniya is an oral language, as writing materials have always been hard to come by in the Sahara Desert. As a result, written transcriptions of Hassaniya sounds into English spelling may vary.

boubou (BOO-boo): a long, wide poncho-like garment that men in Mauritania wear over their clothes.

malafa (moo-LAH-fuh): the beautiful, colorful cloth that some Muslim women in Mauritania wear to cover their clothing and heads when they go out in public.

"Shwai shwai" (SHWAY-SHWAY): "Little by little."

"Wahai" (wah-HIGH): "Come."

"Zaiyn" (zane): "Good."